Horsefeathers!

Woody's ROUNDUP #6

Horsefeathers!

by Kiki Thorpe

Disney PRESS

New York

Printed in the United States of America

First Edition
1 3 5 7 9 10 8 6 4 2

Library of Congress Catalog Card Number: 2001086034

ISBN 0-7868-4461-2

For more Disney Press fun, visit www.disneybooks.com

Contents

1. A Dull Day at Dry Gulch 7

2. An Egg-cellent Discovery! 15

3. Fine Feathered Friend 21

4. Horses of a Feather Flock Together 27

5. The Early Horse Catches the Worm 34

6. Chicken Change 41

7. Pals Forever 51

A Dull Day at Dry Gulch

1.

"**L**ook out, Bullseye!" Woody cried. Bullseye looked up just in time to see a huge drop of yellow paint fall from the sheriff's paintbrush. It landed with a *splat!* right in the middle of Bullseye's forehead. Bullseye whinnied and ran in a circle trying to shake the paint off.

Woody hurried down from the ladder he'd been standing on.

"Sorry about that, Bullseye," he said. He pulled out his handkerchief and wiped the paint off the horse's head. "I'm just trying to get this old jailhouse painted. I thought a new color might cheer it up a little." Woody nodded toward the old brick building, which was partly covered with a coat of bright-yellow paint. As the sheriff of Dry Gulch, Woody was always looking for ways to make the town better. Like planting the flowers outside the post office. Or his "Don't be bitter, pick up your litter" campaign.

Bullseye whinnied again and looked at Woody in anticipation. Usually on a sunny Saturday morning like this one, Woody would climb onto Bullseye's back, and the two of them would go to work. Bullseye might take Woody on a ride out to Rattlesnake Ridge and round up some fearsome cattle rustlers. Or they might patrol the town, keeping an eye out for trouble. Bullseye was always ready to help Woody out.

But this time Woody just patted Bullseye's neck, then started to climb back up the ladder. "I've got to hurry and finish this job," he told Bullseye. "I promised Old Mrs. McNealy I'd help her with her shopping later this afternoon, and you know how she gets if I'm late."

Bullseye snorted and stomped his foot on the ground. He wanted to help Woody by galloping off on some wild new adventure . . . or at least giving him a ride out to see Jessie.

But Woody was set on painting and shopping. He had no jobs for Bullseye. "Thanks, pardner, but it looks like I won't be needing your help today," Woody said as he picked up his paintbrush.

Bullseye sighed. This wasn't the first time Woody had been busy with other work. It seemed that more and more often lately, Woody was fixing a barn door, or helping an old lady across the street, or giving some bandit a good talking-to. He didn't have much time to spend with Bullseye these days. Oh, well. There were other folks in town who might be happy to have a horse around.

Bullseye left Woody to his painting and set off through town to find Jessie. Jessie could always be counted on for a kind word and a carrot. Sometimes she would go for a ride with Bullseye and practice her yodeling, or she would practice her roping, which was even more fun!

Bullseye began to trot as he got closer to Jessie.

He heard Jessie's trademark yodel before he saw her. "Yo-de-lay-ee-hoo!" the cowgirl hollered at the top of her lungs.

Jessie was feeding peanuts to a squirrel that was perched on her shoulder. Nearby, a beaver, one of Jessie's other woodland friends, waited patiently to get her attention.

Jessie winked when she saw Bullseye. "Howdy, Bullseye!" she called. "You're just in time for breakfast." She tossed the biggest peanut in the batch toward him.

Bullseye sniffed at the peanut, then wrinkled his nose. Bullseye didn't like peanuts. He walked over to Jessie and bent his front legs so that she could climb onto his back.

"Sorry, fella. I can't go for a ride now," Jessie told him. "I promised the beaver I'd help him chop some logs. He's building an extension onto his dam, you know." Jessie fondly ruffled Bullseye's mane. "Maybe some other time, fella," she added gently as she handed another peanut to the squirrel.

Bullseye turned and slowly walked back into town. As he passed by Hank's Hitching Post, the general store, he heard someone chuckling. It was the Prospector. He was pushing a shiny new wheelbarrow.

"Hee-hee. Hello there, Bullseye," the Prospector said, still laughing. "Mighty nice day, isn't it?"

Bullseye paused and stomped his hoof on the ground. He was waiting for the Prospector to

put a load on his back. Usually the Prospector wanted Bullseye to help him carry his gold-mining pans down to the river.

But the Prospector didn't even stop today. "No time to talk, Bullseye," he called over his shoulder. "I've gotta get out there and get rich. Today I'm gonna find me enough gold to fill a wheelbarrow. I'm sure of it!" And with that the

Prospector grabbed ahold of his wheelbarrow's handles and headed off down the dusty road toward the river, leaving Bullseye behind.

Bullseye sighed. Woody was busy with his sheriff's duties, Jessie was taking care of her critters, and the Prospector, as usual, was off looking for gold. Everyone had something to do—except Bullseye. Sadly Bullseye lowered his head and began to munch on some sweet grass at the side of the road.

Suddenly something moved in the grass right under Bullseye's nose! Bullseye reared back and saw the beady eye of a snake staring up at him. The snake's red forked tongue flickered out of its mouth, tasting the air.

Bullseye didn't like snakes, especially snakes that interrupted his snack time. With his strong front hooves, he beat the ground making enough noise to scare the snake away. Sure enough, quick as a wink, the snake slithered off through the grass.

Bullseye breathed a sigh of relief and started to nibble another patch of sweet grass. But wait! There was something else lying right where the snake had been. Was it another snake? Holding his breath, Bullseye carefully nudged the long stalks of grass aside. Then he whinnied in surprise.

Sitting among the weeds was a lone brown speckled egg.

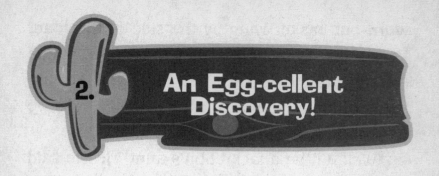

An Egg-cellent Discovery!

Bullseye turned and looked up the road. Then he looked down the road. Could the egg belong to a nearby chicken? But the road was empty—not a chicken in sight. The snake must have stolen the egg from some chicken's nest and carried it to this spot.

Bullseye looked at the abandoned egg. A cool breeze blew the grass around it. Without a mother hen to keep it warm, the egg could not hatch. But what could Bullseye do? He looked around again. This time he spotted an old, worn-out basket lying by the side of the road. Very carefully, the horse used his nose to nudge the egg into the basket. Then he picked the basket up. Holding the handle in his teeth, Bullseye went to find Jessie.

"Well, I'll be a jackrabbit's aunt," Jessie said when Bullseye showed her the basket. "You found a pretty little hen's egg." Bullseye swished his tail happily. Then he turned and trotted into the barn. Jessie followed him. As Jessie watched, Bullseye picked up a mouthful of hay and started making a nest for the egg.

Jessie clapped her hands together. "Oh!" she cried. "You're going to help that egg hatch!" But a moment later she frowned. "You know, Bullseye, hatching an egg is hard work. You'll have to keep it warm all the time. You'll have to watch out for sneaky snakes and rascally raccoons. They'll steal that egg for dinner. And that's only the start. Once the chick hatches, you'll have to feed and watch over it, just like its real mom. Do you think you can do it?" she asked.

Just then Sheriff Woody and the Prospector

came in. "Whoo-whee!" Woody said, wiping his brow. "That old Mrs. McNealy sure had a lot of errands to do. I must have taken her to the general store twenty times today." He stopped short when he saw Bullseye. "Golly, Bullseye, what are you doing?" he asked.

"Bullseye found an egg today," Jessie told Woody and the Prospector. "He's building a nest. He's going to help it hatch!"

"Why that's the silliest thing I ever heard!"

spluttered the Prospector, who was holding the handles of his still-empty wheelbarrow. He was in a bad mood. He hadn't found any gold that day after all. "Who ever heard of a horse hatchin' an egg?"

But Woody shushed him. "I think it's a fine idea," he declared, patting Bullseye on the back. Bullseye whinnied happily and went back to building the nest.

Woody pulled Jessie and the Prospector aside. "You know, I think Bullseye has been a little

lonely lately," he explained to them in a whisper. "This might be just the thing he needs to cheer him up."

Jessie nodded. "It will be something to keep him busy," she said.

The Prospector snorted. "Hmmph," he said. "Maybe so. But I still think it's a lot of durned foolishness."

3. Fine Feathered Friend

For one whole week Bullseye took care of the egg just like a mother chicken would have. Each morning he tucked fresh hay around it to keep it warm. Every night he stayed awake to chase away the raccoons and snakes that tried to sneak into the barn. In fact, Bullseye even tried to sit on that egg to help it hatch!

"No, Bullseye!" Jessie and Woody cried when they saw him. They pulled him up just in time.

"You're a mighty big horse to be sitting on that itty-bitty egg," Woody explained to him. He helped

Bullseye wrap the egg in a warm blanket instead.

Despite the close call, Bullseye wouldn't leave the egg alone for a minute.

"Want to take a dip in the old swimming hole?" Woody asked him one hot afternoon. Bullseye wasn't interested.

"Let's take a ride out to Cactus Canyon to see the prickly-pear flowers in bloom," Jessie suggested. But Bullseye wouldn't budge. He wasn't going anywhere until the egg hatched.

Bullseye's friends were surprised at Bullseye, but they were happy to see him busy. "Golly, Bullseye," Woody said, scratching his head as he watched the horse hover over the little egg. "I've never seen a horse take such good care of an egg before. Well, good luck to ya!"

"Keep up the good work, Bullseye," Jessie said, bringing him a bucket of oats and a big bunch of carrots.

"Hmmph. Durned foolishness," said the Prospector. But he still looked pleased.

And then one lazy afternoon as Bullseye was dozing in the barn, he heard a faint tapping sound. Was it raindrops falling on the barn roof?

No. Was it termites nibbling at the barn door? No. Was it pesky squirrels throwing nutshells at the windows? No . . .

It was the egg!

Bullseye's eyes snapped open. He watched as, with a *tap, tap, tap,* a little beak poked through the eggshell. Then—*crick! crack!*—the egg broke open. Out of the speckled eggshell popped a little yellow chick with a speckled back!

Bullseye whinnied with joy. He whinnied so

loudly that Woody jumped in his chair at the sheriff's office. He whinnied so loudly that Jessie missed the cow she was trying to rope and lassoed the town mailman instead. He whinnied so loudly that the Prospector fell right into the stream where he was panning for gold. All three came running to the barn.

They all watched as the little chick looked around and started to walk. "That is one rootin', tootin' fine-lookin' chick," Jessie said.

"He sure is a handsome little fella," agreed Woody.

"Horsefeathers!" said the Prospector, pushing his hat back off his forehead in amazement. "Who ever heard of a horse hatching an egg?"

Woody laughed. "Horsefeathers! That's what we should call him!"

Bullseye pranced around proudly. "Neighhhhhhhhh!" he whinnied again.

The little chick watched Bullseye for a moment. He hopped on one foot, then the other. Then, to everyone's surprise, the chick opened his beak and said, "Neighhhhhhhhhhhhhhhhhhh!"

4. Horses of a Feather Flock Together

From that day on Bullseye and Horsefeathers were never apart. Everywhere Bullseye went, the chick went too, proudly perched atop Bulleye's head like a cherry on top of an ice cream sundae. All the townsfolk in Dry Gulch loved to see the horse and chick together. Whenever they saw the pair coming down the street, they'd tip their hats and call out, "Howdy, Bullseye! Howdy, Horsefeathers! What do you say?" And together Bullseye and the chick would answer, "Neighhhhhh!"

Horsefeathers looked up to Bullseye and tried to imitate everything he did. He tried to sleep standing up, just like the horse. But the moment his eyes closed he always fell into a heap in the nest. Horsefeathers also tried to eat hay, just like Bullseye. But it didn't taste very good to him.

Other times, though, Horsefeathers was more successful. One day, Bullseye took the chick to his favorite meadow. There were some tasty wildflowers in bloom, and Bullseye wanted a snack. He lowered his head and yanked up a big sweet mouthful of weeds. Horsefeathers watched him carefully. Then he leaned down and pulled up his own snack. Bullseye nodded approvingly. But when he saw what the chick was eating, he almost spit out his food. Horsefeathers was gobbling down a big fat worm! Bullseye tried to get the little bird to eat some grass, but it was no use. Horsefeathers had discovered his favorite food.

By following Bullseye, Horsefeathers soon

learned everything there was to know—about being a horse, that is. He learned how to trot and how to gallop. Before long the little chicken was loping around the meadow like a young colt. He learned that "Giddy-up!" meant "Faster!" and "Whoa!" meant "Slow down, speedy, you're moving too fast!" He could leap over a tree root at full gallop, just as easily as Bullseye could jump a fence. He also knew how to herd a bunch of cattle into a corral, although it wasn't easy; he had to keep an eye out so that he didn't end up under one of their sharp hooves. He even started learning special horse tricks.

"Yee-hah!" the Prospector cried one day when he saw Horsefeathers bucking like a bronco. "Let's enter Horsefeathers in the Dry Gulch rodeo! He'll win first prize!" The Prospector waved his hat over his head, and the little chick whinnied and kicked up his legs again.

But Jessie was worried. "Horsefeathers should be learning how to be a chicken, not a horse," she said to Woody one day. "He should

be with all his brothers and sisters, pecking at birdseed in the yard, not kicking up his heels like a rodeo steed."

"Hmm," Woody said, rubbing his chin thoughtfully. "Maybe it's time we try to find out if this chick has a mom."

Jessie and Woody watched Bullseye and Horsefeathers galloping around the corral. It looked as if they were playing a game of tag. First Bullseye trotted after his friend and touched the chick's tail with his nose. Then it was

Horsefeathers' turn to chase Bullseye. He hopped up and pulled the horse's tail with his beak.

Jessie sighed, seeing the happy pair. "Maybe we should," she said to Woody. "But I haven't got the heart to."

"Neighhhhh!" Horsefeathers chirped into Bullseye's ear early one morning.

Bullseye opened one sleepy eye. It was still dark outside. The sun had not even started to peek over the horizon, and Bullseye could still see stars in the sky. Even the Dry Gulch rooster was still asleep. Bullseye wearily closed his eye again and tried to go back to sleep.

"Neighhhhhhh! Neighhhhhhh!" Horsefeathers whinnied again, louder this time. Bullseye opened both his eyes, and saw Horsefeathers hopping

around and around. The little chick was wide awake and filled with energy! He jumped onto Bullseye's head and pecked at his ears. *Time to get up*, he seemed to say. *I'm hungry, I'm hungry*.

Bullseye grunted. Every morning the chick was getting up earlier than the day before, and he was always hungry. It was hard enough trying to catch the worms and caterpillars Horsefeathers liked to eat, but getting them before the first ray of sunshine reached the morning sky was even more difficult. Being a mom was tough work!

Bullseye gently lowered his head so the little bird could hop down into his nest. Then, dragging his tired hooves and drooping tail, Bullseye set out to find some grub.

Bullseye passed Woody on his way to the sheriff's office. "Mornin', Bullseye," the sheriff said cheerfully. "The early bird catches the worm, eh? Or maybe I should say the early *horse* catches the worm." Woody chuckled at his joke. Bullseye whinnied sleepily.

Woody looked at his tired friend. "Bullseye, you've been looking a little worn-out lately," he started to say. "Maybe it's time you took Horsefeathers—"

But before Woody could finish his sentence, Bullseye suddenly looked away. His sharp eyes had spotted something. Just beyond Woody, crawling up a fence post, was a plump green caterpillar—the perfect breakfast for a hungry little chick! Without stopping to whinny a "too-dle-oo" to Woody, Bullseye took off after the bug.

"Oh, well. Happy hunting," Woody called after his friend.

But when Bullseye reached the fence post,

the juicy little caterpillar was nowhere in sight. Bullseye looked on one side of the post, then the other. He checked the top of the fence and the ground around it. Where had it gone? Then he saw the tubby green grub inching along the underside of the railing. Bullseye opened his mouth to grab it.

At that moment the caterpillar made a sharp left turn and started crawling downward along the post. Bullseye's big teeth just missed the crawler. Instead, they landed on the wooden railing with a loud *thump!*

"Phhhhlattt!" went Bullseye, spitting out a mouthful of splinters. He shook his head and snorted unhappily. Then he looked around for the caterpillar. There it was, calmly crawling south along the fence post. This time when Bullseye got the crafty grub in his sights, he opened his mouth extra wide. . . .

But just then the caterpillar stopped to take a rest. Bullseye's nose hit the fence again. Ouch! When Bullseye opened his eyes, he was nose-to-nose with the creepy crawler. Bullseye looked at the caterpillar. The caterpillar looked at Bullseye.

Then the bold little bug began to crawl again—right onto Bullseye's nose!

Bullseye whinnied and reared! He galloped around the field like a wild stallion, zigzagging this way and that, trying to shake the creeping critter off his nose. The caterpillar held on for dear life, riding Bullseye's nose like a cowboy on a bucking bronco.

Finally Bullseye gave his head a mighty toss and sent the caterpillar sailing into the air. But wait! He needed that grub for Horsefeathers'

breakfast! Bullseye opened his mouth to catch the flying bug and . . .

Gulp!

Bullseye swallowed the caterpillar whole. Feeling a little sick to his stomach and very disappointed, Bullseye turned around and began heading toward home.

Meanwhile, back at the barn, Horsefeathers was tired of waiting for his breakfast. He hopped out of his nest and trotted out into the yard. By now the sun had risen high in the sky. Horsefeathers pecked at a hard little pebble. Not very tasty. He nipped at a dry piece of straw. No good either.

Just then a dark shadow slid across the ground. Horsefeathers shivered and looked up. What could that be? But there was nothing there. Just a bright blue morning sky, filled with fluffy white clouds. Horsefeathers went back to pecking at the dirt.

Again the shadow slipped over the yard, right over Horsefeathers' back. This time Horsefeathers looked up—and saw a hawk diving straight toward him!

Horsefeathers whinnied. He galloped this way and that, trying to get out of the hawk's way. But he couldn't move fast enough. The hawk dove straight as an arrow. Its beak was razor sharp. Its claws gleamed in the sunlight.

Suddenly there was a great thundering sound. The ground shook as if there were an earthquake. It was Bullseye! His hooves pounded the dirt as he charged to the rescue. In the nick of time, he dove between Horsefeathers and the hawk. The hawk swerved quickly, missing Bullseye by a feather. It flew off,

crying angrily at Bullseye for having ruined his breakfast.

Jessie came running up and scooped Horsefeathers up in her hand. She had seen the whole thing. She patted the frightened chick. Then she looked at Bullseye with concern. "That was a close call!" she said. "You shouldn't leave Horsefeathers alone like that. You need to be careful—any mean old creature could come along and gobble him up for breakfast!"

Bullseye hung his head. He hadn't meant to leave the chick alone for so long. Maybe he wasn't cut out to be a mom after all. He started to walk away sadly.

When Horsefeathers saw Bullseye leaving, he hopped right out of Jessie's hand and trotted after him. Horse or not, Bullseye was the only mother he'd ever known.

Horsefeathers hopped up to his usual spot on Bulleye's head. Bullseye perked right up. Together the duo galloped off to the meadow to find some more tasty grubs and weeds to eat.

But when Woody heard the story later that day, he wasn't happy. "Okay, we definitely need to find Horsefeathers' mom," he told Jessie. "That chick might get into more trouble if we don't do something." Woody walked to the barn to talk to Bullseye. Inside the cool barn, he found the horse and the chick sharing a bucket of oats.

"Listen here, pardner," Woody said, placing his arm around Bullseye's neck. "I think it's time you stopped horsing around."

Bullseye snorted and looked at Woody with surprise.

"What I meant to say," Woody tried again, "is that just because you have to give something up, it doesn't mean you're chickening out."

Bullseye blinked.

"Look, Bullseye," Woody said gently. "A horse raising a chicken is a little odd. Horsefeathers needs to be with his real family—with hens and roosters and other little chickens like him. Now, you've done a fine job taking care of him so far. But a horse is a horse, and a chicken is a chicken. And Horsefeathers is turning out to be one strange chicken. Wouldn't it be best—"

But Woody never got to finish his sentence. Before he could, Bullseye walked out of the barn

44

looking sad and confused, only stopping long enough for Horsefeathers to hop onto his head.

Bullseye and Horsefeathers trotted down the dusty lane. Woody followed after them. "Now hold on there, Bullseye," Woody called after his friend. "I sure didn't mean to hurt your feelings." But they didn't get farther than the main road. There they saw something that made everyone stop short.

A mother chicken and her five chicks were crossing the road right in front of them. The chicks were the exact same size as Horsefeathers. And every single one of those chicks had a speckled back, exactly like Horsefeathers.

Woody, Bullseye, and Horsefeathers watched the little parade. When the chicken family got to the other side of the road, the mother hen began to scratch and peck at the dirt there. At first the babies hopped along behind her, pecking up seeds and little bugs from the dusty ground. But soon the chicks began to play. One chick hopped playfully onto her brother's back. Two other chicks played tug-of-war with a worm.

"Those chicks sure are having fun," Woody

whispered to Bullseye. "Don't you think Horsefeathers might like to play with his brothers and sisters?"

Bullseye looked away. Woody stared at Horsefeathers, who was perched in his usual spot atop Bullseye's head. He didn't seem interested in the other chicks at all. But all of a sudden, there was a surprising sound.

"Peep! Peep! Peep!"

It was Horsefeathers! For the first time he was peeping, just like a regular little chick!

"I think Horsefeathers might like to go meet his family," Woody gently said to Bullseye. "Why don't you let him down?"

Bullseye looked sadly at Woody. Then at last he lowered his head so that Horsefeathers could hop to the ground. Horsefeathers looked at the other chicks. Then he looked back at Bullseye uncertainly. Bullseye gently nudged Horsefeathers forward with his nose.

At that moment the hen spotted Horse-feathers. *"Bok!"* she squawked loudly. Quick as lightning, she ran to meet her long-lost chick. Tucking him snugly under her wing, she gently pecked at his head, scolding him with lots of loving clucks.

In an instant, Horsefeathers' brothers and sisters saw him and came running over. "Peep, peep!" they chirped, hopping all around Horsefeathers. They snuggled against him and

pulled playfully at his feathers with their little beaks. "Peep, peep!"

"Peep! Peep!" Horsefeathers chirped back happily.

Bullseye heaved a long sigh as he watched the little bird settle in with his real family.

"Bullseye, that was a very brave thing you did," Woody said. "I know it wasn't easy. Tell you what, I'll take you down to Frosty's for an ice-cold carrot shake."

Woody placed his arm around Bullseye's neck, and the two friends turned and began to walk slowly down the road.

But suddenly they heard a whinny! Woody and Bullseye turned to look behind them. There was Horsefeathers hopping up and down atop a fence post. He flapped his wings at Bullseye. Then he kicked both his feet into the air, bucking-bronco style. He was a horselike chick, after all.

"Neigh! Neigh!" he called. He wasn't letting his friend leave without saying good-bye.

"Neigh! Neighhhhhhh!" Bullseye called back. He kicked his feet out behind him, like the best bucking bronco in the West.

"Well, I'll be doggone," said Woody. "I guess you can take the chicken away from the horse but you can't take the horse out of the chicken."

Bullseye swished his tail happily. Then Woody climbed onto his back and the two raced off to town for a cold ice cream treat.

7. Pals Forever

"**H**ustle up, Prospector. The morning's a-wastin'," Woody called back to his friend.

"I'm hustling as fast as these old legs will carry me," the Prospector called back. "But this dang sack is slowing me down. Why, I reckon this birdseed's nearly as heavy as gold."

It was a bright, sunny day, and the whole Roundup gang was going to visit Horsefeathers and his family. Every member of the gang was bringing a gift: Woody had a bundle of fresh hay for the hen's nest, Jessie carried a new wool blanket to keep the chicks warm during chilly desert nights, the Prospector lugged a big sack that was spilling over with birdseed. And Bullseye carried a basket of fat green caterpillars. He had caught them all himself.

"Dagnabbit!" cried the Prospector as he spilled more seed on the ground. "Git away, ya mangy old birds!" He swatted at two crows that

had swooped down to eat the fallen birdseed.

Bullseye trotted ahead, holding his basket high. Even though he went to visit the chicken family every week, he was excited as ever to see his little friend Horsefeathers. Actually, Horsefeathers wasn't so little anymore. Eating the fresh birdseed and plump worms that Bullseye brought him, he had grown quickly. Now he was almost a full-grown rooster!

The gang soon arrived at the coop where the chicken family lived. Woody leaned over the chicken wire and raised his hat.

"Howdy, folks!" he called.

At the sound of Woody's voice several speckled chickens stopped pecking at the ground and looked up. "Bok, bok, bok!" they called out in greeting.

The Prospector peered into the other side of the coop. "Golly," he said, looking at all the birds. "I can't tell which one is Horsefeathers. They all look the same to me."

Just then Bullseye came up to the other side of the coop and whinnied. When they heard him, all the chickens ran forward to see him, just as

they did every time he came to visit. Suddenly a sleek, handsome rooster dashed out of the chicken house and sprinted through the group of chickens. Galloping like a little horse, he left the other birds in his dust.

Jessie laughed. "Why, that's Horsefeathers right there," she said, pointing to the rooster. "I'd recognize that gallop anywhere."

Woody chuckled, too. "Horsefeathers is one unique bird," he said, shaking his head.

"And Bullseye is one unique horse," Jessie added. She went over to Bullseye and gave him a hug.

Woody, Jessie, Bullseye, and the Prospector watched happily as the chickens and roosters gobbled up the treats they'd brought.

"Well, Bullseye, it looks like our work is done here," Woody said, when the last seed had been eaten. "What do you say we ride out to Rattlesnake Ridge? I hear some lousy cattle rustlers have been stealing cows again."

Cattle rustlers! Bullseye pawed at the ground, ready to go get 'em. Woody hopped up onto Bullseye's back.

At that moment, Horsefeathers leaped across the chicken-wire fence in a single bound. He waited at Bullseye's feet.

"It looks like Horsefeathers wants to come with you," Jessie said.

"Well, why not just this once, for old time's sake?" Woody said. "Hop aboard, little fella!"

Bullseye lowered his head and Horsefeathers hopped right up, settling into his usual place on top of Bullseye's head.

"Now that is one fancy feathered hat for a horse," the Prospector said. The whole gang laughed.

Then, with their heads held high, Woody, Bullseye, and Horsefeathers set off down the road, friends for life.

Your favorite characters are back in this all new rootin' tootin' highfalutin' paperback series.

HOWDY, Pardners

Join Sheriff Woody, Jessie, Bullseye, and the Prospector as they stir up a mess of fun in the wild and woolly West.

Woody's Roundup #1:
Showdown at the Okeydokey Corral

Woody's Roundup #2:
Giddy-Up Ghost Town

Woody's Roundup #3:
Ride 'Em Rodeo!

Woody's Roundup #4:
Fool's Gold

These titles available now at a corral near you

A ROOTIN' TOOTIN' COLLECTION OF WOODY'S FAVORITE SONGS!

An all-new album inspired by the film **TOY STORY 2** featuring the legendary cowboy crooners, Riders In the Sky.

Available wherever music is sold.

Look for these exciting titles from DISNEY INTERACTIVE

Catch the learning buzz with Disney's Buzz Lightyear Learning Series.

CD-ROM

WINDOWS 95/98
MACINTOSH

www.disneyinteractive.com

Disney
INTE
ACTIV